By Malcolm A. Ivy

TERMINAL

"No rain or flood can destroy the structures and work of a man more than the tear that was caused unjustly."

For Franklin

TERMINAL

CHAPTER 1

NOVEMBER.

Surrounded by the warm tint of burgundy walls that wrapped each and every one of them with grace and bliss, there she was, smiling and holding herself. I could tell she was more than lost in the conversation; in fact, she was enthralled with it. I could see the profile of her face, smile gently and comfortably towards her mother. She was interrupted briefly by an ambush of small children running about. The room was filled with the heat of living, and I could hear the husband come over to whisk his bride moments away and just out of reach from her previous conversation. Both of them are hidden from time and space for the duration of their moments together. He was wearing a casual navy shirt with the distinction of a small eggshell-colored tie.

The entire family was there to engage in this wonderful delight. Everyone seemed calm, happy, and eager to await the meal that I could only imagine. The dinner was being prepared in the kitchen just rooms away, ready to serve. The menu is always a surprise to me. What will it be this time, a turkey, maybe even a duck? Who knows, I'm never disappointed.

They're always made with care, love, and tradition. Tradition is what makes the meal work, and it is what has always made the meal work. Never in my wildest dreams have I ever been disappointed by the meal of this family on this day. Oh boy, to my surprise, the doors were flung open from the kitchen, and there I witnessed the goose. A beautiful golden bird lying at the top of a bed of berries and vegetables. Waiting at the end of this table was a father so proud of his wife's creation, ready to cut and carve the bird for his family to taste. Now, he always had a speech, and this year would be no different, but I could never really understand what he was saying. It's hard to believe that anybody could through that smile of his. We deciphered what his lips mouthed as they hid behind his peppered beard. However, I always knew when he was done reciting his words as I saw each of them digging into their plates, enjoying the time spent together, the memories made, and the smiles shared.

The meal at this house and these memories have always been brief, at least to me. It has always been a recurring but fleeting event in my life. Every year has presented itself differently, but it is still the same when narrated by me.

This was my favorite meal. I could only imagine how that food tasted. I could only imagine the smells of that gorgeous burgundy room. I could only envision it all, even though it was before my eyes every single year. However, the weather is cold, and it is best for me to move on from this window, and I will look forward to the meal they serve next year as I peer in.

I began to avert my gaze from the wonderful show; only two inches of paned glass separated the fantastic fantasy of warmth from the cold and somber reality of mine. As I was beginning to shuffle along the blanketed, narrow walkway, the man caught my eye as I was fleeing. I only noticed him for a second, however; I knew in his mind that I would be nothing more than a shadow in the corner of his eye and nothing more than a fleeting memory just seconds away.

I made my way past a couple of houses, and then I heard in the background the door open. To my surprise there was the man, remembering me. He looked at me with a slight grin that could be mistaken for excitement. That being said, I did not turn around to see if that was indeed him. Until I heard my name. The name that everyone in those houses, or even the world has called me. "Hey, you!"

That has been my name for so long that I knew he was only speaking to me. So I turned around in the snow, and to my surprise, he was there standing on his porch with that distinct tie and shirt.

There, for a moment, I thought maybe this was my chance. Maybe he would invite me in so I can finally place names to the faces I have seen over the years. I began to imagine the warmth of a fire and the taste of the meal, and for a moment, I could rest my imagination in the smell of the room. As I began with bright eyes to walk towards the man, either to meet his acquaintance, or to soothe myself from the thought that the world had abandoned me, he began to talk. In fact, he began to shout. He kept repeating the same phrase that only until I got closer did it begin to somber my ears.

"Get lost, get out of here! Go somewhere else!"

"No one wants you. You'll dirty up the place."

I stood there contemplating his actions the best I could. Wondering if this was some kind of joke, it had to have been. Because of my skepticism I began to inch closer so I could gain a better understanding. I had to know for myself, that this could not be what it seemed like.

I drew towards the house and towards the man on the porch. I was still a ways away, hoping, pleading and quietly begging to myself that the mistake being made was from my own confusion.

To confirm my fear was his final statement to me.

"Get off my property, or I'll call the police."
I was not prepared for the wave of emotions that washed over me like the waves of an ocean, destroying the castle built not by any man but that of the innocent child.
What fanned the flames of my emotions was that I could hear the wonderful family inside, laughing, cackling, and encouraging him in his remarks. In agreement, they chuckled at the expense of the man they didn't even get a chance to see but condoned his treatment by others.
I was sad, I was frozen, I was indescribably hurt. All I could hear was their laughing and their enjoyment. Every single one of them.

Those sounds from my misconception burned me to my core, in a fire that was unquenchable. I stood there on the sidewalk hearing their laughter transforming into screams of terror. I could smell the burning burgundy. I could hear the frantic pleading. I could taste the ash in the air. All I could see was the warm glow of the warm home in flames through my frozen tears.

CHAPTER 2

HOME.

This wasn't my first home; in fact, it wasn't my first family. I have been on this planet for nearly 30 years, and I still have yet to receive the invitation. I would like to believe it's from my appearance, or maybe it's because of the knowledge that I possess. Either way, it's irrelevant, as it always has been. The snow drifting past my cheek awakened my awareness of the horror that was unfolding before me. I could no longer hear the screams of the family. Instead, I heard the crackling of the brick, and the glowing embers of the once lived in home.

People began to gather outside of the smoldering building to view this spectacle. Ignoring me entirely as the crowds began to form and outnumber my presence, I quietly and swiftly placed the hood of the coat over my head, and steadily walked in the opposite direction. I can suspect no one noticed me as they never had. They were only concerned about the actions after the cause, and never labeling them as repercussions from the act previously made.

This time of year has never surprised me. The fires have never burned as hot. It always seemed to be different, but never does it happen without reason. I can't control it, I never could in fact. It might not even be my responsibility to control. I have always felt this connection to the world around me, as if the universe selected me to be its soul conduit.

Even as a child, it sounded silly to me, but as I grew older, it became more clear that this could be a possibility. Do I have proof of this? Absolutely not, but without a shadow of a doubt, it is my reality. It's one of those things you know for sure, but, for the life of you, it is something you can never prove. I live in the realm of coincidence and circumstance. This liminal space between power and uselessness somehow has filled my life with more headaches and harm than good. I'm sure if I tried very hard to control it, every single problem I've ever encountered or will encounter would and will never exist.

Why would I try to control the actions of others if they are destined to continuously make the wrong choices? My journey continued down, past the well-lit and wealthy homes of the eastern side. Each house became less ornate, with less gold and ornamentation as I passed. The windows began to shrink, the sidewalks began to get smaller and more cracked. The lights grew far and few after each street.

The roads became dirtier, and the people more friendly as the tents began to sprout. I find myself outside of town, where the burgundy walls were replaced by newspapers and bars. Where the wine and geese were replaced with green bottles and brown bags. Along my journey, I stop at the door of an abandoned building. Surprisingly, it was a bright white door with a brass knob and a small, clear, circular window. Leading to a two-story loft, higher than any building surrounding it. Here was home.

I fiddled in my pockets to find my keys, and with some determination and the passage of time, I secured them. I opened my door and walked up the short flight of stairs. Halfway up the stairs, the door I opened, loudly shut behind me. You could hear the echoes bouncing around the walls, briefly filling the space with life. I was born in this home, as were my mother and her father, but sadly, they were taken from me as my wife and my child were taken from me. As I will be taken from myself similar to them.

There are no pictures in this home to remind me of the things that I've lost, and I have no need for them. I have no need for physical, tangible reminders to invoke the emotion I constantly feel. It is just me in this house, and only me in this house forever. I wonder if after all this, and after me, will it feel any different? Will it be the same as just me in this house? Depending on my considerable effect on the world around me, what would happen? I know something would. I just don't care to figure out why or what. No one else has.

I began to change my clothes for the evening so I could rest to prepare for the day to come. Maybe tomorrow would be better, I'd say to myself as I placed my shoes in the closet next to the rest of my things. I turned on the TV shortly after. To my surprise, 1733 Franklin Ln. was the first thing on the news. It was a horrific fire with no survivors. Women, men, children, nobody made it. The news reporter spoke in a somber and melancholy tone. He discussed the great loss that the community has inherited and how they will surely be missed. The news talked about their charity and their efforts and their missions, that's all they talked about. At least I finally know their names; at least wherever they are, I know they will remember mine. More things happened that day, I soon discovered. There were several fires throughout the county and even some internationally.

This isn't unusual for this time of year. You see people tend to act the same wherever you are, especially if you're like me. I kind of heard enough of the news having witnessed it myself. I decided to make my way to the bedroom for some rest and much needed relaxation. On my nightstand set a bottle of pills prescribed to me from my doctor. I needed to take daily once in the morning and twice at night. I was prescribed that same bottle a year ago.

It wouldn't have done any good anyway. I was told it would make me comfortable, but how can I find comfort? What pill in my mind could forgive the actions of an entire world? Regardless of the symptoms, there is no cure for the illness of reality. So I tucked myself in as I like to sleep on my left side, facing the window, and I thought to myself, maybe tomorrow would be better, or maybe it will be the same. Either way I will be confident either that something would change or I would be comfortable knowing nothing had.

I closed my eyes to witness my anticipated fate. At night when I close my eyes, I do not have the luxury of creating a reality to slip into. I do not have the power to venture elsewhere and let my mind wander as normal people do. My dreams are only memories, and I can only visit them when I'm asleep. My nights are filled with darkness as I lay there with my eyes wide shut, witnessing the eternal nothing.

Only in the morning do I open my eyes as the curtains of the day unfold before me. My reality is the only thing I can create, and unfortunately, my reality is the only thing I can experience in this life or whatever is to come afterward. I glanced out the window, and I could see the birds flocking from left to right outside. I can see the crowded movements of their flapping across the baby blue and speckled canvas. I could see the sun radiating from the corners of my window and casting its shadow onto the floor that crept upwards towards my bed slowly. I could hear the distant radio playing the songs I used to listen to. For a singular moment, I smiled. I smiled to remember how my life was before. Or at least what I had hoped it would be. With each passing second, the joy wrinkling my face evaporated into tears; I began to think of my family; this is something I seldom do, but at times, I'm forced to remember.

I slowly rose from my bed as the sheets clung to my warm body. As I moved about the room, this feeling followed me like a cloud. I took my shower, and I created breakfast for myself as I made preparations for the day. It would be good for me to have a change of scenery. I grabbed my coat and umbrella so I might successfully prepare for my voyage into the streets; although it would be too cold and wet on my journey, I had no other choice but to press on into the elements. As I opened my door, I noticed the small child shoveling the walk in front of my building. He didn't say anything to me. He just tilted his little head and smiled. I've seen him around these parts before, but I didn't bother to know his name. As I walked past him, he spoke to me and wished me a good day. I said thank you, and I hope yours is filled with greatness as well.

He didn't say anymore. He just smiled, tilted his green and white checkered hat, and went about his work as I went about mine. I made my way to a nicer part of town, not too lavish but not as rundown, and I entered a small shop. I frequent the store, but not as frequently as I used to. It was a small bookstore that held the most beautiful poetry in art and literature. Usually, I sit down with a small cup of coffee, pick something new, and I'm always surprised by what I might find next. I walked through the small stoop and I brushed the snow off my shoes and detached my hat from my head. As I took off my jacket in the entryway, the familiar voice of the shopkeep spoke to me.

"Good morning; how's my favorite customer doing? Long time no see."

I smiled slightly in her direction and simply affirmed that it was a good morning. Though I've seen better, I'm enjoying this one so far.

She offered me some new material that came in recently and thought I might want to take a look. I usually read in the back corner of the store where I could be shrouded from the crowd and onlookers who venture to spy on the quiet gentleman who hardly speaks at all, let alone to himself. I informed Susan I'd take them in my usual seat. She said of course and helped me move the stack of material to the tiny table in the back corner. She asked me if I needed anything else, and I confirmed that I did not. She grinned and said to let her know if I needed anything else as she walked back to the front of the store.

She was a nice girl. She always kept her to herself and tried her best to make everyone feel comfortable. There was a time when she wasn't that great at it, but everybody needed a little practice over time, right? We all don't get it perfect from the start. It takes some time to work on yourself and succeed.

I looked down at the stack of books and found some interesting titles amongst the pile. The one that caught my eye was titled. "Lost, the Story of Home."

I paused for a moment as I contemplated the title. 'Lost: what is the point of describing a place you are unfamiliar with? What's the point of trying to define it? It's a state of being, not a place. Most people are constantly lost, while others waste their entire life trying to get lost. Some people are even born lost; it's the nature of humanity. In fact, I think it's the only true nature of humanity.' I read a couple of lines from the first page, only to deepen my understanding of how long I could get lost in this reality. My true home is to be lost. I took a sip of my coffee and felt the warm, soothing drink flow downward.

I looked through some of the books until I finally landed on a book about nature. I'm someone who enjoys the clarity and serenity of nature. I think it's the best thing anyone could experience. It's very soothing, in fact, if you think about it. Surrounded by life and earth, it gives you a sense of calm. In the midst of my discovery, I heard the bell of the bookstore door, signaling a customer. I heard a familiar voice. It rumbled and gargled its way through the shop, asking for the finance section. I knew exactly who it was, and from the looks of it, I was correct. In fact, it was my old employer. He worked for one of the banks that I used to. He was a tall man with circular glasses and a head full of thick black hair. It was unusual for me to see him outside of a three-piece suit.

Even in casual wear, he dressed fantastically. He was a man of many talents; however, the only one he exercised and practiced religiously was firing people. I would know because that is exactly what he did to me a couple of years back. Part of me wanted to go over there just to lay eyes on him, but I decided to leave it alone and return to my books. He caught my eye and made his way towards the back of the store.

My quiet little corner was loudly interrupted by the towering man.
"Well, if it isn't Mr. No-Show himself, how's it going?"
It took every ounce of my being not to strangle this man, but I was cordial enough to address the conversation.
"I'm good, Harold. How are you? I'm just doing some light reading."
He looked me up and down, then glanced at the piles of picked-through books in front of me and continued in a smirky tone,
"Some reading, huh? Well, good thing I gave you all that time."

I couldn't believe what I just heard. Every bone in my body began to contort and twist and crack unanimously. I felt the boiling rage from such an idiotic remark. I took a deep breath in and out and remembered this is my happy place. I gathered myself internally and smiled at him. Knowing exactly what could happen, I chose better.

He continued to say, "Oh, I'm just joking with you. You'll land on your feet; I know it."
I smiled and nodded and wished him a good day. On his way out, he gathered his books that were sitting and waiting for him to check out, and then made his way to the door, where his hat and scarf were located. I went back to studying my books, as my time was starting to end anyway. However, I heard

Harold at the front door wish everybody a good day, including me. Specifically, in my direction, he said,

"Tell Marilyn I said hello."

He finished putting on his coat and calmly walked out the door. I was so filled with shock, anger, and sadness all in one. I couldn't believe I just heard that name. How dare he say that name to me, of all days and of all the places in the world. There was absolutely zero reason for him to not remember. I sat there, frozen, as the book fell from my hand. All I could see was the closed door and the echoes of a small bell.

I couldn't stand to think about what had just happened. There's so much emotion these days, and I am not sure if I am capable of handling it. I need to just go elsewhere. I left everything on the table and gathered my things to leave. This place has been ruined for me, and now I am more lost than I've ever been. I swiftly thanked Susan for picking those out for me and exited the store in hopes of something better.

As I pushed open the door, the cold air hit me like a wave, its chill piercing through the turmoil inside. The streets, once bustling with life, now seemed like a surreal painting, each figure moving in a blur, uncaring and unaware of the storm raging within me.

The city, with its familiar corners and echoing sounds, felt strangely alien, a jarring backdrop to the whirlwind of emotions I harbored. In this moment of wandering, the world around me morphed into a reflection of my inner chaos, every step leading me away from the bookstore but not closer to any real destination.

It was a poignant realization of how my identity was so entwined with the memories of places and faces I once knew. With each aimless step, I delved deeper into my thoughts, searching for a peace that seemed as elusive as the shifting shadows of the town around me.

CHAPTER 3

ROUTINE.

I tried to have a better outlook on the remainder of my day, knowing that I had a more pressing evening planned. Today was the day I went on my final interview for two positions. The first one was the one I was hoping for, and the second one was a last resort. I finished up my cup of coffee, trying to shake off the encounter I previously had and realign my mind towards a positive outcome. On my walk, I made it to the bank in hopes of retrieving my position. I looked at the doors, adjusted my tie, and tried to fill myself with a sense of false courage. I stood there for a moment on the steps of the building, and then I entered through the double brass doors. There I saw the beautiful red marble floors and the white alabaster columns that adorned the hallway. I looked down at the notes in my pocketbook that listed the room number of my appointment. However, there were three separate hallways that were vaguely identical to one another. This was enough to confuse me when trying to go in the right direction. I saw a security guard, and I asked if she could help me find my way to room 114. She rolled her eyes and slowly but casually strolled in my direction to look at the notes I had printed out previously. She looked at the paper and then back up at me. In an elevated tone, she remarked for the whole hallway to hear, "Are you blind? You have to go down the first hallway. Those rooms are designated 100 through 120."

I tried very hard to compose myself internally. The only thing that I could mutter was, I'm sorry. She rolled her eyes again and went back to her post as if I was completely bothering her. I took my things and went directly towards the door. I don't know why I was nervous as I walked down the hallway. The worst thing they could say is no. I'm not concerned that's what they might say, but I'm concerned that's what would happen. No one deserves to be disappointed, especially when they need something the most. So I calmed myself as I walked down the hall, and the numbers began to increase. I was on the search for the room I was looking for, which I finally did. I knocked hesitantly on the door and waited for someone to greet me. I knocked once more, and finally, I heard a voice. "Come in; we're ready for you." I decided to open the door and have a seat. The room was a robin's egg blue and a nice walnut table sat in front of the young man with bright red hair. "Please have a seat, Mr. Astor." I made my way past the double chairs and sat on the far left, greeted him, and politely shook his hand. I dropped my bags on the floor and placed my hat on the opposite chair.

"It's a pleasure to meet you" he said, with a distracted demeanor. He began to shuffle some of the papers on his desk and search for my previously submitted application. As he was sorting through the jumbled mess, I tried my attempt at small talk. "It seems to be very busy around here."

The man hardly looked up from his desk as he was still looking for my resume. He only paused to briefly murmur, " Yeah, we're overworked and underpaid here."

He then smiled with a faint chuckle as found my crumpled document. He quietly, but obviously examined the parchment, and seemed to be too polite to acknowledge that it was not in the best condition. He then looked up towards me, and we began our interview.

"So tell me a little bit about yourself."

I explained to him some of my credentials from my previous work and then explained some of the references I had. Mid conversation, he stopped me and asked me about a pause I had in my work history. Then went on to say that this gap seemed quite a bit long and an untraditional length of time. Every cell in my body was hoping that it would not have been an issue and that he would simply not ask the question I dreaded every single day, but I had no choice but to answer his request. I went on to explain that the reason for my three-year hiatus was a direct result of a death in the family. The man laughed a bit but caught himself to realize that I was not trying to be funny, and in fact, that was an honest and realistic answer. He pardoned himself for his reaction but inquired about the length of time.

Emotions that were so deep within me were swirling and brought to the surface. I further explained to the man that not only did my wife pass away, but my child as well. In an accident that was extremely preventable. I had a hard time dealing with the loss of my family, knowing full well that I would never see them again.

The man sat back in his chair with a melancholy look. This is a look I've seen before from individuals who know what they should say but don't know how to go about it. It was the face of awkward understanding. He assured me that he fully understood, and sometimes that's just how death works. I replied to him, knowing better, "That's not how it is supposed to be."

The phrase puzzled the man, and he frantically tried to switch gears back to the interview regarding my work. We sat for another five minutes of him, asking me more about my credentials and my past experiences. I tried to the best of my ability to successfully go through the questioning. Towards the end of our meeting he leaned a bit closer on his desk and said things I was preparing to hear from the beginning of our conversation.

"Mr. Astor, thank you for your time today. However, it's kind of a difficult fit I fear."
He genuinely sighed and slumped back into his chair, trying to find a more articulate way to further his conclusion.

Feeling that this conversation would end this way, I shortly interrupted him asking was there anything in my resume that made me an ill fit for the position?

"Oh no, no no no no it's not necessarily the credentials, it's more of the nature of the matter."

I now see that I have graduated to "a matter" instead of "a problem". In fact, I'm quite proud of myself for not going back to the commonly used "issue" that I seem to always be.

I heard more about what he had to say and listened intently, knowing whatever he said, and however, I felt would not have actually changed a single measure of my current situation. I softly gathered my things and thanked him for his time, and for his consideration. I shook his hand, and predictively shuffled towards his door.

And right as I reached for the doorknob, he stopped me.

"Wait!"

I stiffly turned around only to sadly catch his eye, anticipating his next obvious comment. The next words, out of his mouth, were a bit odd. In fact, if I may be frank, it seemed quite stupid.

"Do you like music?"

He asked me as he looked at the left corner of his desk.

I met his response with a swift "Yes, I do; in fact, I am quite fond of music. Why do you ask?"

His eyes perked up a bit as if he were about to participate in some good deed that day. "You may not have a place here, but I do know a place for you." His smile began to grow bigger and more frightening with each word.

He began to tell me of a nice store that his brother is in charge of. He thought there would be no issue in giving him a call and telling him that I would be a perfect fit.

My eyes began to water, knowing that this might be the saving grace I'd been looking for. In fact, it might be the next chapter of the story.

He did have to warn me that the hours are odd, and the pay isn't the best, but it's something. Maybe something could come from it.

He told me to wait right there and have another seat on the couch next to the door. As he called his brother, could hear him on the phone, confirming that he was indeed looking for someone to watch the store and help stock and things of that nature. I could hear the sigh of relief that the man on the phone gave his brother as if he had single-handedly answered all of his prayers. As I was sitting there, trying not to look like I was eavesdropping on their conversation, and falsely decoding the crappy 90s corporate art on his wall, I noticed the man give me a thumbs up, and a smile, trying to signify to me that it was a done deal, and his brother would interview me.

I tried to be as calm and collected as possible, but inside, I was absolutely relieved. I felt like something could really come of this. Even though it's not what I set out to find, it's something that I found along the way.

The man hung up on his brother and began to give me a little more detail about the position. I asked him if I needed to interview and when I would need to schedule a conversation with the man.

He spoke at me with an eager tone, saying

"No need, you're hired just like that."
He snapped his fingers right next to his cheek.

He gave me the address and sent me along my way.
I thanked him so much, and I shook his hand at least five different times as I walked towards the door of his office. He wished me luck on my travels and closed the door behind me. I was so excited to hear some good news that day. I began to dream about how life would start to look better. How there was hope left in the world, I was excited to be a part of it, I was so thrilled, in fact, that I forgot my hat in his office. I willfully made my way back down the hall towards his door, and as I

started to open the door, I heard that he was on the phone again. I knew that it would be extremely rude for me to just burst in on him as he was having another meeting, so I fixed my hand to knock. Just as I was about to make contact with the door, I heard him laughing, and I began to listen.

"Poor idiot. His resume was hot trash. There's no way in hell I would expose him to our workers. Astor is an HR nightmare. At least you can take them off my hands. I did the world a favor, I guess…Call it charity."

I could hear that they both started to laugh, and I realized that not all gifts are pleasant. I backed away from the door and walked down the hallway to the main entrance, leaving my hat behind. Maybe he will get better use of it. Maybe the hat will find more kindness from his words than I ever could. I was happy and grateful for the opportunity, but saddened by the vessel it appeared in. That's all I can be for this gift, is grateful. Maybe one day, I will find a gift or an opportunity where I am both grateful and happy at the same time.

CHAPTER 4

REPEAT

I began to walk towards my next destination, knowing that I had limited time to get there. I looked down at the card he gave me for the address, and it wasn't but a few blocks north of here.

I haven't actually been on this street in a while, but I have passed it many times. It was situated on a street with several small businesses like dry cleaners and small restaurants. Places that I have been to before, but I haven't been in a while. The street can bring so many unwanted memories for me. The memories that they do conjure up are beautiful and yet hauntingly tragic. I decided to do a little bit of people watching as I walked towards my next stop in life. As I was walking the concrete road, I saw a man, and who I presumed to be his wife, smiling at his conversation. They were holding each other close as their eyes lingered into one another. They seemed to not have care in the world. They were holding each other's hands so tightly. Almost as if they didn't, the other would slip into oblivion. Not that that's true necessarily, but it was very real to them. Which goes to show that it meant a great deal to The couple. It's a beautiful thing to take care of someone other than yourself, unnecessarily and selflessly, without hesitation. There's nothing in life that I would trade to experience such magic and beauty again.

Behind them, I saw a father walking with his young daughter. She couldn't have been more than six or seven years old. I saw her skipping along the path, clumsy, bumping into her father's legs, without an ounce of grace or humility. I could see from her father's gentle grimace that his shins would never be the same as they had met the forceful kicks of a skipping young child. I can tell in his eyes, through the pain, that there was love, compassion, and patience. I stopped to kind of think about what I witnessed. Something in particular really grabbed my attention about that statement.

Patience. That's something I've only been asked to give and something I have never in my life not even once received. Patience is something you should be gifted, not necessarily something that you should be forced to provide.

As I thought about it a little more, not everyone can have patience. Patience is a luxury to some that others do not have the privilege of providing. Because with patience and the ability to practice it, one must first have time. Time is something I cannot afford to waste and, for sure, something I cannot give away for free. Society asks you to be patient, and society considers it a great virtue. However, it ignores the fact that time is a commodity that's withheld from so many people. Sadly, those are the ones whom the world asks to provide patience in abundance for others.

I continued on my path as I neared the destination. The storefront was like any other store. There was a glass window and an open sign, but nothing out of the usual. It was nearly 6 o'clock that evening, and the wind began to pick up. I went in through the revolving door to witness a partially crowded, half-empty music store. I could see the man behind the counter eagerly looking for what I presume to be his new employee. I was looking around to see if he would notice that his new employee had arrived. On second glance, he met my eyes with

a surprised and wide-eyed
demeanor.

"Hello! It's a pleasure to finally
meet you; I've heard great things
from my brother." He said.

I tried to play along, knowing full
well that his brother had only shared
insults and the opposite of kind
words in regard to me. I went on to
agree with his greeting. He began to
show me things around the store. He
laid out the schedule and said that I
would be working more of the night
shifts, unlike the rest of the
employees here. I went on to ask if
there would be anyone else on this
shift with me. He swiftly shot that
down and assured me that I would
be the sole person on the later shifts.

I would be responsible for making sure everything was neat and tidy, as well as organizing some of the records that would be misplaced throughout the day. He asked me about my organizational skills and I told him I was not only a quick study, but extremely proficient. I love making plans as you can see even if they don't always work out. He chuckled nervously, but continued on with his grand tour.

He explained to me, the different locks and keys that were associated with each lock. He couldn't stress the importance enough of making sure that the store would be locked at night. I asked him if there were any security guards or bars that he put on the window. He looked at me and said that's not in the budget. Most importantly, it wasn't something I needed to worry about for someone in my position. I told him that I understood, and he shook my hand and said welcome aboard. I thanked him for giving me an opportunity as I had anticipated to provide a more formal thank you. However, as he patted me on the shoulder while still holding my hand mid-shake, he said our family loves to do charity work, and we're always happy to help someone in need.

Even though he sent out the smile, I couldn't bear the amount of anger surging through my body. Knowing fully that the only charity that these people provide for those in need are the ones that can help them in return. Nothing with these people are ever out of the kindness of their heart I fear.

"Yeah", I swallowed my pride and continued shaking his hand, expressing the fake gratitude that I had accumulated over the last hour.

As I was filling out some of my onboarding paperwork, I saw someone in the corner of my eye. She was very familiar with her overly recognizable smile and laugh. I noticed that it was Susan again. She was surfing through some of the classical music. I was very thrilled to see her so I decided to place my tasks aside to go say hello and have a small chat. I walked up to her and she was still nose deep into the album. I tapped her lightly on the shoulder and said, "Susan, it's me."

"Mr. Astor," she exclaimed, "how are you doing, and what are you doing here? I've never seen you here before."

I smiled as she leaned in for a small celebratory hug as if she hadn't seen me recently. I explain to her that I was doing quite well. In fact, I started my new job here today. I'm gonna be keeping the place all neat and tidy and making sure no bad guys come to destroy the place. She said you're the guy to do it and she slightly laughed out loud. This is one of my favorite places. I'm a huge fan.

I noticed that she had a stack of vinyl as thick as a dictionary. All of which were different types of music like Mozart and Beethoven.

I asked her if the music was all for her because I didn't actually take her for a classical lady. She shrugged and said, "Actually, for someone else. I wasn't sure which one they recommended. Can you kind of help me out here? They are a little bit on the young side."

She smiled graciously, still carrying the stack of music.
I looked through what she had already picked out, and I selected one that I thought was the best.

I said "Claire De Lune was one of my favorite songs. I think you should go with that."

She placed the heavy stack down and picked up the one I was holding. She was so happy that I could help her. However, out of the corner of my eye, I saw my new employer staring holes into both of our clothes. I could tell that he felt this conversation was happening a bit too long. He swiftly but nonchalantly levitated towards the both of us and in a high-pitched voice. "Was there something I could help you with?"

"I don't think so. I was just chatting and discussing music. Thank you, though."

She smiled sarcastically. He then went on to suggest that our employees aren't here to make conversation. They're here to help with music and sales, and a good employee would do well to remember that.

Saying that, he glanced in my direction, still smiling, but his eyes were not. I told him it wouldn't happen again and that I would do better next time. Susan then interrupted me before I finished my statement and said, "He was helping me plenty; it takes two people to figure out one problem."

She glanced over at me and verbally thanked me for my assistance. She then walked towards the cash register to make her purchase, but not before she said. "Thank you, Astor, for helping me. I really do appreciate it. I'll see you around some more. Don't forget to stop by the bookstore I have some new stuff for you."

She smiled and walked past my boss.

The two of us were standing there as she disappeared towards the back of the store. He then looked at me and said, "Don't let that happen again. You're not here to make conversation. Do you understand me?" I told him yes, I understood him very clearly. As he began to start wrapping up for the day, he doubled back and said.

"Your name is Astor? My brother said your name was Greg. Let me go and change your name tag."

I was shocked to see that he couldn't even have the decency to ask for my name. All I am to people are what other people choose to call me.

He then went on to say the unimaginable. He asked me if I wouldn't mind being Greg for about two weeks or so because he already ordered the name tags, and it might be too expensive to change them now.

At this point he can call me whatever he wants. I'm not here to make friends. Apparently, I'm just here to sell records. At least it's a start. So, I stood there at my post as the commotion and bustle of the store began to die down. People started to leave the store, and the last remaining stragglers, one by one, vanished. I organized some of the records and stocked the incoming inventory for the next day. It's not much; in fact, it's not what I've dreamed of doing, but at least here, I might find peace. Most people like me have the right to ask for more, but for someone like me in my current predicament, I am comfortable asking for less in exchange for some ounce of tranquility. I will do my best to maintain what little I might receive. So, I wrapped up my duties, gathered my things, and prepared for my humbled walk home. In the process of gathering my coat, I almost forgot to lock up and set the cameras. Immediately, dropping my stuff at the door, I went back into the service room urgently to arm the system. I put in my password and turned on the cameras. The system was so crappy, as my boss had mentioned before that it took a couple of tries to get into the system. Minutes went by, waiting for this archaic software to load. As minutes turned into an hour or so, I finally saw the blinking red light on the camera in the corner of the storefront flicker on. "That must mean it's working," I said to myself, "it's not the best system, but it will have to do." I then fumbled for my keys as I headed toward the door. I grabbed the rusted lock that my boss provided me to lock up the store. The lock was a heart shaped mechanism well past its years. It looked as if it would only take one small drop of rain for it to shatter into a cloud of orange, metallic dust. I thought to myself, "This would be a lovely opportunity to invest in this storefront." I knew that I had a lock similar to this one at home. Now, of course, it was not in such a terrible condition as this one, and it was a different shape, but anything would be better than this. I gently secured the chains and went about my way home. It was dark and very quiet during my walk, and hardly anyone was on the street, a sprinkle of people every now and then, but nothing noticeable to the average person. I really took to heart how Susan visited the store, it's always pleasant to be in her company as well as it is unfortunate to be in her absence. She was the type of person that made you feel extraordinarily normal. She carried herself with a sense of hope and optimism that spoke volumes on the busiest of streets. Her confidence radiated to the point of contagion, leaving you sick with pride and joy. I knew a woman like that years ago, whose personality was just as potent but no longer lingers in my system. It is refreshing to remember as well as being reminded. The thought of these women carried me further into the night, towards my home, where neither of them waited but were always welcome. It was a crisp still night, void of motion, and its silence hovered over me like a dense fog, lingering waist high. I finally reached the steps of my home and threw myself into the entryway. I took off my shoes and tossed them to the corner. Not in any particular way, but just enough to imitate care. I clutched onto the banister tightly as it guided me up the stairs to our bedroom and as I prepared for bed and began to drift away, I thought I faintly heard laughter from down the hall. I rested peacefully, disregarding reality, and found comfort in the memory.

I woke up the next day in a different tone of being. I felt, for a moment, honestly eager. Usually, the day drags on before it even begins, but as of this morning, it feels fresh. The sky had not a single cloud in sight and was as blue as the ocean. I showered and groomed myself and prepared for the second day of my new occupation. I made a small cup of tea for breakfast as I applied the finishing touches to my appearance, but noticing the clock on the mantle, I'd rather be on time than full. I thought to myself now is not a good time to create bad habits of punctuality. So I removed the teapot grabbed the lock I set out the night before to replace the old one, and began my route to work. On my way to work I saw the same people as I always have roaming to and fro in the town. I saw the same smiles and frowns of the people passing by, and for a brief moment, I recognized that I was one of them. I came to the realization that life has its ups and downs; it's not about where you've been; it's about where you're going and how you got there. Crappy things may happen, but not forever, like I noticed that someone shoveled my walkway this morning in front of my home. Not perfectly, of course, but an attempt was surely made. I'm looking forward to the day I am going to have and the effort I am willing to spend on it. As I was nearly skipping to work, I began to see commotion outside the store. There seemed to be a small gathering of people standing in a circle around the entranceway. As I began to get closer, I noticed that they were police officers. I could tell by their long, black trench coats. In my mind, I thought that someone must have gotten hurt or even passed out in front of the store. I even thought maybe it was a bank robbery, not that I had hoped for it, but wouldn't that have been interesting? The distance between me and the storefront shortened by each step until I met the men face to face. Part of me just wanted to go in and let them do their thing. However, the other part of me was curious and wanted to ask what had happened. So listening to my more creative and insightful side, I struck up a conversation with one of the officers. I asked him, "What happened here? Is everything alright, officer?"

He looked up from his notepad and said, "There seems to have been a huge break-in and robbery at the record store." My eyes widened, concerned for the safety of the store and everyone in it. I asked the officer, "Is everyone okay? Did anyone get hurt?"

He said, "Everyone was fine; this happened last night; the owner just seems pissed." My heart sank into my chest, leaving me with the feeling of the inevitable reality I was sure to face. I made my way past the guards, measuring and taking photos of the broken glass of the revolving door, and I could see the disintegrated chains of lock swinging off the door. When I entered the store, I saw the wreckage. There was glass, water, and broken records everywhere; standing in the midst of the chaos was my boss. He was frantically talking to the officers waving his hand about viscously until he caught my eye. His face melted into a deformed disgust growing every wrinkle on his face. He pounced toward me aggressively with anger in his eyes; all he could say was, "What did you do?" I looked at him, shocked, as I, too, was surprised by the events around us. I said I didn't know and asked what happened. Through beads of sweat that jumped off his face, he explained that someone, in the middle of the night, had simply entered the store and wreaked havoc, and we are pulling up the tapes now… "If you have anything to say about all of this, now is the time." I looked puzzled for a moment until I ultimately realized that he was accusing me of the damage. Not only was I being accused of doing it, but I was also being accused of potentially lying about it. I began to stutter and trip over my words in an attempt to explain myself. "I didn't do this," I said frantically. "I did everything you told me to do; in fact, I tried to do more. I reached into my bag to pull out the lock. "I knew that the lock was rusted, and I brought a new one." My boss wasn't hearing anything that I was saying. He was so blinded and deafened by his rage that he willfully ignored every explanation I provided. The police shortly came over with the video evidence, and we all gathered around the monitor. For a while, we only saw the grainy footage of the storefront until we saw three figures, one with a bat, enter from the left. The figure with the bat was a short person. We saw him reach for the chain, open the door, and then proceed to walk in and destroy the place. Shortly after the damage was done, they left the place just as quickly as they arrived. One of them dropped something on their way out; it looked very familiar, and so I looked over my shoulder to the left of the store, surrounded by caution tape and the forensic team; I saw it: underneath the glass and rubble was a checkered hat. The same hat that I saw shoveling my walkway days prior. I was in shock, I couldn't breathe, I couldn't speak, I simply couldn't. My body stiffened through shallow breath as I turned back to the scene; my boss looked at me, and I could hear the words he was about to mutter. He looked at me and said, "You had one job, and from the looks of it, you couldn't even do that. You didn't even lock the gate; what is wrong with you?" I fell to my knees onto the broken glass that sprinkled the floor, knowing the only words to linger on my lips were "but I did." Those words floated in my mouth unable to escape knowing they would never reach the ears of the man I needed to hear it. So the words evaporated from my mouth in the same fashion as if I were to say them aloud. The man, through my silence, uttered the obvious horror. He said a lot of things that I couldn't comprehend, but what was certain was that I was fired. That is the only statement that lingered in my ears, like a ghost returning to its grave. I opened my mouth to conjure up the spirit of my emotions and all that I worked for and placed myself beneath my true value and below his feet, and I begged. I begged for his understanding, I pleaded with his humanity, and I threw myself at his mercy, and what I was met with was the silence of his heel pressed into my chest, knocking me from my knees to the ground. So I lay there, on the damp, sharp floor, frozen, until I felt the cold hands of the officers grab my hand and pull me up, and they dragged me across the floor, through the wreckage, toward the street. I lay there, knowing they grabbed my hand and lifted me higher from the dirt, only wanting to let me fall further to the dust. So I lay there, weeping in the cold January air, finding sweet release in sleep at noon.

From the feeling of sharp glass to the feeling of biting cold, I woke up blanketed by snow. I could feel the pain of my feet vibrating through my body. I looked down to see that my shoes had disappeared, and my watch as well. Sitting about five feet away from me was a homeless man who noticed I had awakened from my slumber. He told me about how some people in the middle of the night had stolen my shoes, my watch, and my money. He then reassured me that they left the wallet. Through my frozen tears, I asked, "Why didn't you stop them?"

Without hesitation, the homeless man said. "How does helping you feed me, clothe me, house me? Whether I let them take your money or do worse, I will still be here." I was so shaken by those words I stared into his eyes, and I saw his life. I saw all that he needed and all that he wanted, but I was willing to look past all of that in search of all that he feared, and I showed him those things. Every fear he ever had and every fear he will ever experience. I sat with him as he experienced every single one of them until his eyes blackened in pain. As he slumped

over, I felt his heart slowing. So I
did my absolute best to make sure
it beat on, as long as I needed it to.
I knew I was numb from the
horrors I had recently experienced.
He will have to feel them for me.
So I got up from the street, and I
walked toward my home, barefoot,
in the falling snow.

CHAPTER 5

CRUMBLING.

Placing one foot in front of the other, I continued my trek home, shivering more from the actions of men rather than the cold, falling snow. The same walk I took this morning has transformed into a death march to an early grave. I found myself wandering aimlessly toward my comfortable place. I have lost so much and sacrificed everything to gain little to nothing. I have the wounds of a battle well fought without the trophy to remind me of my victory. Hope has abandoned me yet again, and joy has only visited my heart for a brief moment, only to swiftly leave me gasping for more or something at all. Though the snow was falling down and my mind clouded, it was clear to me that nothing in this life was worth living for. Life is only livable for the past and never the present. I live for dreams and memories. I am a person who has given everyone so much; in fact, I have given them more than they truly deserve, but I am always spared the courtesy of kindness. It is quite clear to me that the only thing hope is good for is a return to the past.

I continued walking as the snow began to blacken my feet, and I arrived yet again at my home. As I climbed each step, I thought of an important lesson that was taught to me and a lesson I have tried to teach. Today is for figuring out tomorrow so that tomorrow is better than today. I try to remember that; more importantly, I try to remember the face that told that to me. I try to remember what, and how she said it. I miss my wife, and I miss my son, and I guess I hope what I do today is always enough for tomorrow. I may walk it alone, but I do it for them. There are still good people in this world. I have to believe this. Otherwise, there is no point in moving on or forward. Between the tears and hardships, maybe hope can warm my heart and comfort me, as she once did. I continued to walk up the stairs and began to fumble with my keys to the door, and as I began to push my key into the lock, the door creaked open.

It swung slowly inward to reveal the sight. The floors were smashed, the glass was shattered, and the once regal home was stripped bare. All the art was ruined, all the wood was damaged, and the place was left unrecognizable, as left to the care of animals. I walked through the door in shock, gasping for breath and understanding; there were no words to describe this. A lump formed in my throat as I quickly searched for the essentials. I ran to my bedroom to find important papers gone or torn, I stumbled to the bathroom to see my medicine cabinet wrenched from the wall, empty and discarded in the bathtub. My medicine, the one thing I desperately needed to live, was gone and crushed to powder under the foot of these burglars. I do not know what happens when I die, if my emotions cause such a violent response from the world around me. I have not allowed myself to think of the outcome of my demise, but now, both the world and I are facing it quickly. A deep sadness was unleashed within me, accompanied by chariots of rage wielding anger on my soul. I searched through each room and the valuables within. As I combed through the relics of my home, I discovered they were unsalvageable, except for one which was the most important, a silver box.

This box was special to me. It was a gift from my mother that was gifted to her by her father and so on. It's been in my family for a very long time. A medium sized box with a simple polished finish, was not ornate or fancy by any standards, but was enough to care for. The top was cracked and there was a hole on the side big enough to see through. It was beautiful before, but now it will never be the same.

I was upset that someone could do this, of all days. The respect for me and my home, and all that I have built, the countless years I have put into my life, and the memories made meant nothing to the select few who decided the worth of my works. My very life smashed before my eyes in shambles on the floor around me. I was enraged and fueled by malice. I kneeled to the ground and shook my fist. I began to punch the floor with all of my might, again and again and again. I continued ruthlessly and consistently; each blow was like a heartbeat leaving my chest. The sky began to turn black as I beat my emotions into the ground until the floor began to crack. However, I continued without cease, and at each blow, the crack grew bigger and wider to the point that the building itself was shaking. I fell through the floor, and the building collapsed on top of me.

Unrestrained by physical limits, I kept punching as floors, concrete, and rocks gave way to my wrath. I beat on tirelessly until there was nothing left. It felt as though the earth itself shook with anger beneath my feet. The ground began to violently shake as I continued to beat away at the ground. Broken physically and emotionally, I stopped to look at my hands, which now were covered in blood.
The bones of my fists pierced through my skin, a physical reminder of the raw wounds unable to heal. As I inspected my hand, the ground continued to rumble as the

sound of earth colliding, crushing, and reforming took place. For a fleeting moment, I wished to stay where I was and lay myself to rest. To hopefully find peace underground with my family and the life we built together. I wanted to stop fighting; why should I keep fighting when everything told me to be right here where I belonged?

Yet, again, whether for the respect of any tiny scraps of innocence left in the world or a simple stubbornness to face what happens after this life, I decided I could not stay. I quietly wept for the family I mourned, and for the horrors, I am sure to witness. Once all was still and the earth fell silent, I crawled through the ruins of my life, scraping and peeling the skin from my hands as I reached toward the light above me. Removing every rock and boulder from my path, I crawled toward an idea I no longer believed in for reasons unknown to me. My dark fallen cave began to brighten as I pulled myself upwards toward the surface. I reached my torn hand to the sky, now able to feel the sting of the air hitting the raw bone of my fingers and pulling myself up, above the shoulders, where I let out a loud, thunderous cry that shook the very ground as well as my core.

I could feel the dust enter my body through every breath, and I could feel the ash lingering on my exposed flesh. I pulled my body free of the rubble, and I stood to my feet on top of the hill that was once my home, and I released a guttural scream, the kind of yell that leaves you breathless, yet you continue to scream, void of air. All that I knew was reduced to cinders beneath my blackened feet, and I could hear the screams, the horrible screams. As I looked around my fallen castle, I could see the same fate for others. I saw the entire city leveled in an instant. I saw the lives of thousands reduced to mounds, and I could hear the ones trapped beneath the weight of their worlds, and for one small moment, they were with me.

CHAPTER 6

US.

Through the wallowing sounds of the now barren wasteland. I had finally seen what I've done. I was no longer blinded by the pain that I was enduring and I recognize the horror I have caused.

The sky was gray, and the sun that shined so vividly was now hidden behind the clouds of destruction and debris. The snow that once covered the manicured streets now lay beneath a layer of soot and human architecture. It was only made possible through grief and hurt. I somberly walked and slid my way down the pile and walked through the destruction all around me. I was surrounded by a garden of hands and symphonies of screams, begging and pleading for help. I am just one man, and there are hundreds of hands grasping, not necessarily for me, but for anything. I started to help them. I started with one hand and then another. The first person I helped escape from the heap was a young boy. He was bruised and scratched up from his falling down. His eyes were swelled with tears, and his hands and arms were bloody. His clothes, resembling cloth that has been weathered by storms of dirt and rain, covered parts of his body. As I pulled him from the rubble with my naked, stripped hands, I looked at him, thinking how sorry I was to put him in this predicament. His entire life came crashing down not from anything that he did but because of my actions. He had his whole life ahead of him to achieve and accomplish wonders. What have I done?

Hopefully, by saving him, I could make it right. Hopefully, in time he can forgive me. He stood there, catatonic, watching me tend to my garden of suffering. Not moving a muscle, he stood there watching it all unfold, dead but still breathing.

I frantically began to search for other hands and try to pull them from the ground. I started to grab them and pull them to the surface. More and more, they became aggressive and frantic and climbing over one another, trying to escape the pits of life in this hellish landscape.
The desperate people were like animals, crying and clawing and pulling their way to the top of the heap

for breaths of air. There was a crowd that began to form from the gathering, the crowd began to push me and shove me in all directions, and I was knocked to the ground. They trampled on everything in their path in their agitated frenzy. There was no longer standing room for me. I tried to claw and crawl my way on the ground out of the stampede of people. In the middle of all the chaos, my hand got caught in all the commotion and was trampled on.

My hand sat there motionless on the ground, severed from the rest of my body. A surge of pain galloped through my body, hitting all corners of my being. When it finally hit my mouth, I exuded the loudest yell imaginable.

During my deafening scream, the ground vibrated from the Earth as the clouds circled above and gently crashed to the dirt. The winds poured from every cell of my body in a hurricane of power, the crowd of people flying in all directions as the wind that was knocked out of me, collided with them, only to be brought down to earth by the tear, exiting my face which summoned the heavy rain that pushed them downward shortly after.

So I was not alone in my pain, but I was alone in my hurt. With my remaining hand, I clutched the small box tightly to my chest, knowing well the only gift I have ever been given now is the only thing to comfort me in my loneliest and darkest hour. The innocence I was asked to guard and cherish no longer exists. The gift was nothing more to me than dirt in the field. The box no longer shined or sparkled as it used to. It was no longer perfect. Or was it ever perfect? I asked myself, fighting back the tears I had cried.

This gift has plagued me beyond recognition.

I can no longer, in good conscience of my own best interest, possess this gift, nor should this gift ever be inherited. Is it my fault? Am I the one to blame for this? Should I have done something different or at least something better? Should I have forgotten it? Should I have kept it? Should I have accepted the gift? I have ruined it. If I am not here to protect it, then surely the only thing I have left would vanish entirely, and what would be my purpose?

More importantly, I asked myself if I have truly failed like I have, does the purpose exist?

I pondered for a brief second to remember my purpose. I had to search deep within myself to find it, but after some contemplation, it presented itself to me. My purpose, whether I do it flawlessly or not, is to be here for people in every way I can and in every way I am needed. So, I gathered myself, gently placed the silver box into my pocket, and removed myself from the chaos swarming around me. It started with a slight jaunt to the left and quickly escalated to a sprint. Madmen were running about the place as if on fire. I began to reach the edge of the commotion where the stampede died down, and I started my walk to greener pastures; the chaos vanished behind me as the pleasantries grew more numerous. I found myself walking the same cobbled streets I'd walked months and years before. It took some time to get here, but eventually, I did arrive. I began to see that the nicer parts were not severely hit, in fact, they were thriving. I continued walking some blocks inward to find some people who would be willing to help me. The houses began to get more elaborate and sizable as I walked further into the neighborhood. I could see some of the people strolling about on the street with their families and friends. I saw some walking their dogs and playing with their children as if the destruction miles away didn't happen. They were enjoying the beautiful weather without a care in the world or for it. I could hear laughter and good feelings from almost every corner of the avenue. I felt as if I had walked directly out of one horror movie and straight into a scene from an American classic. I was like a fish out of water, standing on the docks, watching the seas boil to my left and miles of picnics, lunches, and pageantries to my right. Hearing from one side the cries of a million fish jumping out of the steaming waters to catch the cool, crisp air on their scales, to alleviate the scalding pains they can't escape. While witnessing the joys of hundreds of people flocking to the sands to catch the summer heat for fun. Then there is me, in the twilight, torn between two realities that shouldn't exist but coexist.

I continued to walk past the well-cut lawns and clean streets that made me second-guess my reality. Was all that had happened back there a dream? Did it happen? For a moment, I thought it hadn't. People started to notice how out of place I was, and who could blame them? A limping man in tattered clothes, filled with dust and blood, and minus a hand. They all seemed disgusted and appalled when gazing at me. Not because of my appearance but more due to my presence interrupting their manicured moments. My existence bothered their aesthetic. I kept walking until I reached the town hall and proudly entered the building. As the door swung open, I could see all eyes shifting from their current tasks to my face. I then could see their pleasant faces turn to scowls of inquiry and discomfort.

I hesitated shortly, feeling all the eyes settle on my body, and for a moment, I was engulfed in sharp judgments, similar to when one enters a space not dedicated to you. Like arriving to a dinner late and uninvited but begrudgingly present. That energy swallowed my mind and surrounded it briefly like the warm, frothy sea, kissing the shores and swiftly receding. My mind focused not on the state of my function or lack thereof but on the needs of those whose screams still echo within these halls, even if I am the only one to hear them. Carrying on, I allowed the dust and debris to trickle from my clothes onto the alabaster-marbled floor, and with every step, I could feel the dry, caked clothes cling and rip from my wet and bloodied body. I could see the people, as I walked past, eager to insult and defame but hesitant to act on their thoughts and feelings towards what they were witnessing. Their true demeanor presented itself as only two things, visibly uncomfortable yet physically silent. I reached down in my pocket to feel the outline of my sliver box, reassuring it's proximity on my person.

 I held my head with confidence through the wrenching pains of a bruised and battered body. I began to approach the Victorian, ornate, and gilded doors of the mayor's office. The door stood tall with its gold fixtures and crystal glass complimenting the burgundy pine wood. I could feel the small stream leak down the exposed bone of my hand, dripping in sync with my limping footsteps onto the polished floor. Leaving crimson dots paginating my steps. This time, without forethought and regardless of pomp and circumstance, I barged into the office.

As the door flung open, the laughter and chuckles of the room filled the hall as well as my ears. I could see the mayor surrounded by his cabinet, abruptly stop at this unprecedented sight. Their long, porpoise-like faces stared at me as they sat at their round table. They began to look at one another to see if anyone had answers until the chatter ceased when the mayor spoke.

He smiled in a familiar grin. "Hello Astor, its quite a surprise to see you here, but not a surprise to see you like this." Standing there in the frame of the door, trying to hold myself up, I asked for a seat which he offered shortly after. I sat at the end of the table while they clustered with each other on the other side. He asked what my purpose was here, and I informed him of what had happened. I described to him the pain, the suffering, and the demolition of the society not far from here. Before I could go further into vivid detail, he made it clear that he was aware of the tragedies. In fact, everyone was aware of the earthquakes and floods.

I was filled with joy, knowing that we were not alone and not suffering in silence. As a tear dripped down my face, cleaning a path to my chin, I began to inquire about plans and resources to help. However, I was interrupted once more by a sharp and guttural… no.

Looking perplexed, I thought I had explained the situation incorrectly, so I repeated myself and was yet again met with the same response. In my confusion, I tried to understand how and where the interpretation was getting lost. The cabinet, after viewing my facial response, began to giggle and nudge each other in a humorous and playful manner at the expense of my confusion. The mayor stood up and the commotion of the room died down as all eyes were now on him, including mine. He said in a calm and matter-of-fact tone. "You see, Astor, we are well aware of the issues plaguing that district. We are also well aware of the horrors those citizens are causing themselves.

We've always known that those people were capable of such monstrous things in times like this. Many of us here, singlehandedly could help, but why should we? Why should we doom the lives of these good people here, who have no say or right in the actions of others? Only to assist those people who doomed their own by choice, and choice alone. As I look out this window right now I see a paradise, I see wonderful homes, I see families. I see a beautiful world worth saving. Why would I expose my citizens to that? Is this not a paradise? There is no pain nor hunger, no sadness or hurt. It's perfect, you wanted it this way. In fact, you're the person who helped us build this. You've done the impossible, Astor; why destroy it?"

I was speechless, and nothing could stop me from knowing that what he said was true. As I tried to look through my tears at his face, he went on to say. "There's this poem that I think you might know, and it goes like this if I can remember it correctly.
"I wish to be far away enough, where the bombs are nothing more

than a gentle breeze on the shores of my luxury."

The room fell empty as I knew he was only talking to me. It was silent, as I grew beside myself. He continued to talk saying "She was right to say it, and it's a shame she never got to see it. So thank you for all of your help, we could not have done all of this without you."

I asked him, "What are you going to do? Nothing?"

Then one of his cabinet members interrupted me with a smirk and a raised hand "Actually, on the contrary, we have taken measures that would bring a great deal of help to many a people. The moment we heard of the atrocities, we promptly reallocated the funds and banks resources in that district, reevaluated the inventory of pharmacies and hospitals, as well as the inventory of produce and grocery establishments."

I said that I was relieved, that this would, in some way, help them. Or at least it was a start. The room once again filled with joyous laughter and an eruption of cackling. The mayor, composing himself as if just hearing a great joke, said while wiping away tears of joy, "Astor, not them… Us."

CHAPTER 7

EMBERS.

Those last words were the only sounds I remember, as I must have blacked out. From my arrival at that building to the slow and dismal shuffle down the steps outside, I remember nothing. I hardly remember the transition from point A to point B having my mind entirely focused on the state of this world and those who reside in it. Slowly and without urgency, I walked back to what remained of my home. From the previous conversation and the ones surrounding me now, that home seemed to be the only one worth knowing. On my long travel back, I walked down the street that was familiar to me.

It was the house with the burgundy walls, or at least it used to have the burgundy walls. The charred wood and black soot no longer adorned the brick. Instead, it was a completely new color, as well as its interior, a complete restoration, and currently for sale. I saw there, placed along the fence, was a solid gold plaque that said in bold font, "No Loitering." Even here, they can forget the tragedy but only remember to blame the cause. I reached into my pocket to feel the silver box, and it seemed to gain more dents and cracks than I remember. It seemed to be falling apart from the seams gradually over a short period of time.

Then it hit me, a revelation unlike any other; it was one of those thoughts that had passed your mind previously, but you paid no attention to it at the moment. Like a bridge that one would cross at a later date when they had gotten to it. Now I stand there, mentally at the bridge I have been trying to avoid or ignore for years. The epiphany was made clear to me more than ever before. I've unwillingly but truly, come to the conclusion that the gift was a curse. The world I was given to live in and create was a mistake. It was a terror, and one could never find peace here. Sadly, not even me; I have done and seen great things, but hope in this place borders the realm of impossible and unlikely. The words trust, chance, and righteousness towards all men here have evaporated into four-letter words. I witness this paradise with its birds and blue skies, only to realize it is all for show. Behind every flower, beneath every pond, and inside every home lurks the lie. The illusion of humanity is a contagious one that presents itself without symptoms that prey on the kind, the wonderful, and the willing, and it had captured me.

  Why bother with the cure, I question as I feel the crumbling box in my hand; why should one even make them comfortable before their passing? Comfort is reserved for the helpless, the weak, and the vulnerable. This world is nothing of the sort and is the complete opposite of what is needed to deserve such peace. I exited the town as the gates closed behind me for the last time. The magic within me no longer yearns to escape, and for the first time in my life, I tended to myself. For the first time, my body clung to life, not out of necessity but out of want. For the first time in my life, I felt something outside of hurt, sadness, or pain. I felt anger, and it felt good.

The sky winds slapped the clouds about in the air toward the same direction in which I was walking, still shuffling along the roadsides. Not a single car occupied the streets, and it was me with nature. I began to enter my town covered in ash and destruction. I searched long and hard to find any traces of humanity, only to continually confirm my solitude. It was a graveyard of life, and it was hard for me to recognize a dead idea. I passed my home, still the crumbling mound I left it, and I took a moment to take the box that I cherished and set it at the foot of the heap. The moment I sat the box on the ground, much like the building, it collapsed upon itself. As if recognizing its final resting place and instantly returning itself to the earth, from which it came. Life is designed to fail because life attempts and pretends to last. With nowhere to go and nothing to see, my shoeless feet guided me back to the last place I might find an ounce of authenticity.

I drifted through with what little energy I had left. I rounded the sidewalk, now showered with remnants of the nearby buildings, I moved my exposed feet carefully around the large chunks of concrete, and support beams collapsed in my path. As I approached the street with the bookstore, my view was obscured by a semi-truck that had been abandoned in its ruined state. The trailer blocked the street and was tightly wedged between the remains of a pharmacy and a clothing outlet. With no way through, I gently lowered myself to the ground on my stripped and only hand and inched my way under the trailer, little by little with my elbows serving as my method of progress. My legs dragged behind me with the weight of my journeys. As I came up from the other side of the trailer, I kept my eyes sealed shut, and it was too much to imagine what horrendous scene might await me.

Would the bookstore be in ruins? Would anyone be among the

debris? I gathered my strength as I got to my feet, and finally, with tremendous effort, I peeked through my eyelids; I saw the scattering of books that transformed into piles as I assessed the remains of the store. Scavenging through the wreckage seemed pointless since the covers of page-less books fluttered through the air as the smell of burning paper hung heavily around the hill. Not having the strength to crawl back under the semi, I continued down the street. I did not know where I was going, every landmark disappeared from my memory and my sight. It was only after what felt like an eternity that I heard the jingle of what seemed to be pots. The sound faintly grew and materialized as a woman carrying pails of something and walking in my direction. The figure was confidently yet cautiously walking toward me. I went further into the open street to make myself visible as well, and with great success, the person saw me. They paused for a moment, and began to rush forward with increasing speed.

With each passing second, the figure became more familiar than before. The woman began to grow features as she hastily stumbled. To my joyful surprise, it appeared to be Susan. She was carrying what looked like pails of water on both of her arms. She looked as if she recognized me. I began to wave and shout at her, but she remained silent. With each shout I gave she looked more and more concerned as she sprinted towards me.

I continued to grab her attention verbally until I saw her drop the buckets of water. She started waving her hands in the air frantically as if she was trying to signal me to do something. I shouted back at her, "What? I don't understand." I then saw her shake her head and place her finger to her mouth in a shushing action, I then realized that she was asking me to be quiet. Finally understanding, I quietly raced to meet her. She hugged me tightly, only to stop after my noticeable wincing; she backed up gently and examined me from a short distance away. She noticed that I had been badly hurt and that I was on the verge of collapsing. I was physically in a bad place, my hand still dripping, and I stood there silently. My appearance spoke for itself. My severed hand still dripping on the ground toward my blackened feet. Her eyes welled with tears as she began to help me to a safer location. She said to me in a quiet tone. "I'm so happy to see you, I thought you didn't make it. It's nice to see a familiar face." I asked her about the bookstore, and she assured me that everyone got out ok, and they relocated to a safer area. She explained to me that it was not safe to be out in the open like I was. She told me about the looting, murders, and horrific scenes that had happened while I was gone. "They just turned into animals." She said. "They started with the innocent, and the easy. Then as time went on they graduated to vulnerable people. First they attacked the neighborhoods and the small clusters of people trying to find refuge. It is just a horrible place here." She finished.

I could see she was starting to get choked up, so I decided not to press the subject any further. She changed the subject by asking me how I was doing. It was hard for me to answer as I walked past the destruction of the streets I used to know very well. I could hear in the distance small bursts of screams and popping sounds. She looked at me, kind of puzzled, suggesting that those sounds were new and that we had to keep our heads on a swivel, walking through this new world of ours. I've never seen her like this, nervous and in shock. While she was fumbling in her bag, she pulled out a stick of gum from her purse. It was bright, neon green, and smelled like apples. At least, that's what she said it smelled like. It was her last piece, and she wanted to offer it to me. I refused, and she placed it in her mouth and began to chew. As she was blowing a bubble, she paused after seeing a man run across the street in front of us. She told me I would have to be careful, sometimes they ambush, and sometimes they just want to get to a safer place. We continued to talk for a while on our way back to the place where she was staying.

"Where are you guys staying?" I asked.

"The library, it wasn't hit as hard as the bookstore I worked at." She said. "My apartment's gone too; otherwise, we could have stayed there." My stomach turned, knowing the cause of all of this was my doing. She continued on. "It all started so fast, the store was shaking, and we took cover. After the tremors subsided, we dug ourselves out little by little. The fire department did come help us in the beginning. I think that was the last time I saw any first responders…” She trailed off. “Sorry, Astor, it’s been a while since I’ve slept; I’m a little unorganized. After being dug out, I went to go find my husband since the phone lines were down. I raced to his work as fast as my feet could carry me. Praying and hoping for everything to be alright. When I got there, the building was leveled, and no one was around to help me. I had to hope he was out to lunch or forgot something important for one of his meetings.”

“Did he?” I asked with caution in my voice.

“He did.” She pursed her lips. “I raced home, and I found him and his secretary in bed. So engaged in their horrendous affair that neither of them realized earthquakes had leveled the other parts of town."

"Susan, I'm so sorry". I uttered. "You didn't do it, Astor; you don't need to apologize. Anyways, the storms that followed were what affected our apartment. The whole building swayed under the tempest that followed. Knowing the building couldn't be safe to habitat after, we all evacuated. I didn't know where else to go or what to do, so my husband and I went to find a safe place to stay. We didn't really have time to discuss any of it. I'm so angry, I'm so mad at him and I'm hurt beyond belief, but I love him, and everyone makes mistakes, even the ones that hurt this deep."

A small tear fell from my face as she was talking. Whether it was from the pain of my disintegrating body or the realization that through all of this tragedy, love can exist. She tried to smile through her grief, though she was terrible at lying. I honored her attempt and comforted her in the best way that I could. She was carrying me as we hobbled to our next destination, and I clung to her tightly and embraced her to let her feel welcomed and loved. From that, she knew, at least with me, she felt loved. The night started to emerge from the dark orange sky and we started to pick up the pace, because of safety concerns. As the sky became darker, we noticed a faint orange glow in the distance. I saw that Susan's face became more and more concerned as we approached the small glowing ember in the distance. The closer we got, the slower we walked until it reached an inevitable halt. Only then did I realize that we reached our destination.

CHAPTER 8

PEACE.

The library was burned and still burning. The wood was etched with glowing embers. All that remained was the simple structure of the previous building. I could tell by the level of destruction that there were no survivors. I saw Susan walk into the building, and I followed her. The groans and popping of the building echoed its nonexistent halls. The bodies littered the floor like leaves on a crisp fall day. I caught a glimpse of Susan standing in the corner, vigorously staring at a spot on the floor. I could only assume who she was staring at, so I politely made my way over there to comfort her. I felt it would be unwise for her to be alone in a moment like this, with a loss this traumatic. I grabbed her shoulder and leaned her into my arm, but what I found was even more chilling. I saw the crackling corpse of her husband in the corner of the room, wrapping his arms around the smoldering corpse of another woman, possibly, to my knowledge, the same woman. The only recognizable piece of him was his wedding ring. I knew this feature to be true because his wife was wearing a matching one. We stood there for a while in silence. In her moment of silence, she raised a trembling hand and removed her wedding band engraved 'Faithfully Yours' and gently placed it on the hand of his lover. Her face was puffy from crying, and she calmly said, "Here, Margaret, I'm glad you were there for him." She stood and wiped her eyes. She turned to me with a sincere smile, saying, "At least he wasn't alone, and at least he was at peace and happy, and I'm glad I wasn't there to ruin his happiness in his last moments." She grabbed my shoulder and helped me out of the building. Now that there was nowhere to go, we camped out at an abandoned warehouse near the wreckage, which was still glowing late into the evening. We both finally found some rest in faded office chairs in the small workspace above the factory floor. Susan had brought some of the surviving books from the library and was using them, along with some lighter fluid, to create a small campfire in a metal trashcan she found. As she prepared some small cans of food she had in her bag, I asked her, "Why did you take off your ring?"

She hesitated as the emotions drummed back up inside of her. "Because bad situations aren't forever, I loved him, and we built a life together, but the pain will fade, and I will move on. Leaving the ring with them felt right. It is not serving me any good to hold onto it besides reminding me of how we said goodbye." Her eyes settled on my arm, and with surprise exclaimed. "Oh, I'm sorry. Let me bandage you up! There's got to be a first aid kit in here." She started to rifle through desk drawers. "Here it is!" She said identifying the orange case fastened to the wall. "It's going to be painful, but I need to clean your hand and cover your other arm too. I thanked her as she sat beside me, working diligently on cleaning my wounds and covering them. She had the lightest touch, which made the cleaning that much more bearable.

"I can't imagine what you're going through," I said. "Well, I can understand losing a spouse; what I can't understand is how you are handling the betrayal."

"I don't really know. I didn't look at it as a betrayal; I think I saw it more as an incompatible situation. It didn't make it hurt any less, but it allowed me to focus on the situation rather than the people involved. If you don't mind me asking, did you go through a divorce?" She asked.
"No. My wife and son died."
"Oh, I'm sorry. I didn't know," She stammered.
"Thank you, but you wouldn't," I replied, "in fact, I think that this is the first time I've talked about it in a while."
"I couldn't imagine losing a child. That must have been devastating."
"It was and is, but my wife wanted me to keep going; I find comfort in trying to make tomorrow better than

today. It's one of the only things that has gotten me this far."

"I don't mean to pry, but how did they die?" She asked very quietly. I paused for a moment; how do I explain it? The situation was very complicated and I don't think I can bring myself to explain every detail. "They died from a terminal illness, the same one I have," I responded. The weight of confessing it made it that much harder to handle. I held back my grief. It felt like I fell into a pit that was swallowing me whole, but I looked into her eyes, and I knew I needed to finish my thought. "I only have a few months to live, and that's ok." I lied, putting on a brave face for her. "I'm dying and it would have been extremely sad to leave this world having not seen kindness again. Yet you did; you showed me the truest and most profound sincerity. If there were one person that I could save from this whole mess, I would save you, maybe the only person around who is worth saving. So thank you for showing me again that kindness does exist." We continued talking through the night, about everything. The conversation itself cast out beams of light, which kept the darkness at bay, with even more impact than the fire that crackled between the two of us. While my mind was alert, my body was weary, I had difficulty moving my legs, and I had lost all sensation and movement in my feet. My feet felt dull and hollow. As dawn broke, I saw Susan perk up suddenly. "I have a surprise for you. I almost forgot about it until now." She said as she hopped up. "I'll go and get it for you."

"Let me go with you." I said. But my feet only twitched slightly as I tried to get out of the chair. "Nonsense. You're injured and need rest, and I don't know how much longer you could have kept going like that. Besides, it's just across the street. I'll be back in just a moment." She swept out of the room quickly, held her head high, and walked with a purpose I hadn't seen in her since yesterday morning when we met. I tried my best to watch her out of the window as she crossed the street and back into the library. I counted the seconds she was out of sight, each creating a sense of unease in me. I watched a man run across the street and stand in front of the doorway. He seemed familiar. I strained to see where I knew him from. I squinted hard and racked my brain. Then it struck me, he followed us, he was the man from yesterday, and he knew Susan was in there alone. I banged on the window to get his attention as one, two, three, four, five, six more men showed up each taking a stance in front of the library exit. They now formed a semi-circle around the steps leaving the building. I slammed my hand against the glass with everything I had. Screaming at the top of my lungs, I watched desperately as they set their trap. I tried standing up to race out the door, but my legs wouldn't support my weight. Whatever I had done to them, they were no longer of use to me. I glanced out the window, only to catch motion inside the building. Susan was walking toward the door. Through tears streaming down my eyes, my hand bleeding through the bandage, as I slammed against the window, I screamed. I screamed in hopes that she would hear me. That she would run and get away.

She walked out of the front of the library and froze; the men approached her as she started to back into the building. One of the men grabbed her and pulled her forward, ripping the bag from her shoulder. Two of the men gathered around her and started beating her viciously as the man went through her bag, dumping the contents onto the ground. There was nothing, she had left the food and first aid kit here with me. Viciously, he tore open the gum container she still had there, only to find it empty. Frustrated by finding nothing, the man from yesterday signaled to all of the men by dragging a finger across his neck that he decided her worth, and there was nothing left to take besides her life. The men beating her drew something out of their pockets, and with a flash of steel, I wailed as they plunged their knives into her chest. I had to do something, and with a grunt of effort, I kicked my chair over to the door, where I flung myself down the stairs. Feeling every step connect with my body, I held my breath, hoping desperately that this fall wouldn't kill me. Not out of fear of dying but because Susan deserved someone to come to her aid. When I finally hit the cold, unforgiving concrete floor. I heard the snap of my ankle. There was no time for screams, and the pain needed to wait. I looked up to see where the exit was. Using the final traces of strength I had, I drug myself toward the door, bleeding from my hand and my severed arm; dragging along useless feet, now bent at odd angles from the fall, I inched along the floor. When I finally made it out into the daylight, it shined with a cruel intensity. I saw Susan lying on the steps of the library, taking shallow breaths, and her cruel tormentors must have delivered a fatal blow to leave her to die. I crawled my way across the street and gently cradled her neck with my forearm. I yelled for help. I looked up and down the street for anyone. I yelled again, and when I felt Susan's fingers come to my lip, she was shushing me. Her eyes, full of pain and fear, rasped, "Help us." As her hand shakily moved mine to her stomach. All of the air left my body as I deflated. Looking at her, I knew there was nothing I could do.

I held her close as my body racked with sobs. I couldn't help, but I wouldn't let her die alone. It was only a few moments before she passed, but it stretched into what felt like an eternity. I looked into her eyes as she finally let go. I felt her strength leave as that spark left her eye. I wept and gently closed her eyes. Her heart, which had been beating as though it carried the torch of humanity through this cruel world, was finally snuffed out, and her body felt lighter for it. I finally pulled back from her face to look at the sky, mocking; not a cloud was around to witness the loss of humanity's kindness. The single woman who saw goodness everywhere she went has now cast her gaze elsewhere. I heard a clink, the sound of metal scraping rock, and I looked down to see her hand clasped around something. I gently opened her hand to see what it was.

The small disheveled silver box. The same one I left.

From that moment I knew it was time, I never thought I would do so willingly, and I never thought I would be alone when doing it. Yet here I am comfortable with the decision, there is nothing left here, realizing the world died the last time I saw my child's face. So I joined her, in the place where they linger, waiting for me.

CHAPTER 9

TRANQUILITY.

Light filled the room, drenching reality in the purity of nothing. I heard my footsteps before I saw myself walking toward Susan who was sitting on the bench. My footsteps echoed through the empty void until I finally reached her. I sat next to her and she looked up at me and we hugged. I asked her how she was feeling and she replied saying "I'm not. Not to sound cliche, but comfortable."

I leaned in closer and said, "May I ask you a question? This might be the most important question you ever answer because I can only ask you once."

"Of course, I'm ready," she replied. I leaned in close and asked her the question "What do you want?"

She smiled and took a moment to make sure that her answer was the truth, and with great confidence, she said. "A paradise I deserve."

I gave her a soft smile, and made exactly what she asked for, but before I did, I asked her something I've never asked anyone before. "Could I join you?"

"Of course".

She then vanished from my sight, and I appeared back on the street where I had last seen her lying on the ground. I stood up and walked toward the sunset. It was so beautiful; with every step, my body grew lighter and lighter until I collapsed into dust like sand falling to the ground, where I returned to the earth I was given. The moment the last grain of my being fell, the world stopped. The world began to vibrate, and a hum filled the air; the trees began to unravel from each branch, and the world became smoke. The sun, suspended in a permanent twilight, setting on the world men created, never to rise. In the streets where men burst into flames and men drowning in the tears of their victims without the sweet release of death, never to die. Men in the middle of the street transforming into pure gold. You could hear their screams as people began dismembering them for their riches and where the hands of thieves were reduced to rotting flesh, never able to grasp the contraband. Everyone is busy, frozen in time, doomed to repeat and endure the actions that they have committed to others. The feeling of starvation, never to be satisfied, and who would hear them if not me? I could hear the screams of the world. I heard them all. Every single person I knew and every single person I didn't. I left them with the gift of life. I left them with the world they created. It was time for me to go. My body couldn't handle the weight of the world. So I left this world to its own.

Somewhere distant, at some far point in time, there was a house flanking a beautiful street; it was a quiet street, and the snow blanketed the walkways gracefully curving around every corner. Sitting inside the window of this house was a woman playing with her daughter. The child was running about the place while her mother chased her around the dining table, surrounded by the warm tent of burgundy walls. The weather was quite chilly; snow fell, littering the windowsill outside; it was so beautiful. There was a gardener tending to the red roses covered in snow; he was naked, with no shoes or shirt, but he was only wearing a hat. The gardener always looks into the warm home, but he has never been inside; that is why Astor keeps the windows open so that he can look in. The child noticed the man outside in the cold and asked Astor, why does the gardener keep looking inside our home? Should we let him in? Astor, still looking through his book, remarked, saying that "The actions that man took only spared him from the horrors of that world. It is nearly a charity for him to be where he is now". The little girl smiled and continued to play about the house as she ran off disappearing into the home. Susan walked over to Astor while he was sitting in the chair next to the fireplace, reading his book titled "Lost, The Story of Home," and listening to music. She asked him if he wanted anything from the kitchen, "I'm about to go make a snack for Jane." Astor looked up from his book and said I was just about wrapped up this book anyway. "I will get that started for you." She smiled and went to find her daughter. Astor got up, passing the skinny side table that sat across from his chair. Placed on top of the marble and brass table was the small silver box with a hole in it. Astor walked passed the table and

went into the kitchen. Jane appeared shortly after in search of her mother and Astor. She ventured into the living room, where she walked past the silver box. As she got closer to it, she could hear the screams of millions of people crying out in torture and begging for help.
Astor re-entered the room to inform her that her mom made some snacks.

Jane asked Astor if he could hear that. He looked puzzled but smiled and asked her to clarify what she meant.

"The yelling and screaming… from this box… can you hear it?"

Astor smiled and kneeled down to her level to explain to her that sometimes he does, and sometimes he doesn't. He said to her in a gentle voice, "Your mom and I come from a wicked place. A place where evil happened to people who didn't deserve it. So we created a paradise and closed all of those bad people out so they could never get in. Sometimes they get mad that I'm ignoring them. So I placed them in this box to think about what they have done."

The girl smiled and understood what Astor said by adding her own commentary that made sense to her. She said, "Is it like time out?" Astor chuckled a bit and affirmed, "Yes!

Exactly like time out". Jane asked how long they were in time out, and Astor shrugged his shoulder, saying, "I'm not sure, and long as it takes them to learn, I guess." Jane giggled and ran through the kitchen door where Susan was actively listening. Susan thanked Astor for breaking it down to her in an appropriate way. Astor smiled at her, knowing he had tried his best not to traumatize the child. She said to her softly, "My reality is filled with their screams of help. I should be the only one to hear them. I won't burden her with their cries". Astor asked her if he had made a mistake in torturing them for eternity in that box. Susan smiled briefly and told Astor, "Life is about choices; we all have the choice to do something or nothing at all. Has helping them ever brought you peace? Astor understood and locked the box indefinitely.

Astor created a paradise for him and the girls, and they lived in bliss as they forgot the hell they left behind. The snow looked so peaceful, and for once, so did he.

—— End ——

www.ingramcontent.com/pod-product-compliance
Lightning Source LLC
Chambersburg PA
CBHW071324140726
47996CB00005B/1813